Sleepover Girls

See Stars

by S[...]

Collins

An imprint of HarperCollins*Publishers*

The Sleepover Club ® is a
registered trademark of HarperCollins*Publishers* Ltd

First published in Great Britain by Collins in 2000
Collins is an imprint of HarperCollins*Publishers* Ltd
77-85 Fulham Palace Road, Hammersmith,
London, W6 8JB

The HarperCollins website address is
www.**fire**and**water**.com

3 5 7 9 8 6 4 2

Text copyright © Sue Mongredien 2000

Original series characters, plotlines
and settings © Rose Impey 1997

ISBN 0 00675504–6

The author asserts the moral right to
be identified as the author of the work.

Printed and bound in Great Britain by
Omnia Books Limited, Glasgow

Sleepover Kit List

1. Sleeping bag
2. Pillow
3. Pyjamas or a nightdress
4. Slippers
5. Toothbrush, toothpaste, soap etc
6. Towel
7. Teddy
8. A creepy story
9. Food for a midnight feast:
   chocolate, crisps, sweets, biscuits.
   In fact anything you like to eat.
10. Torch
11. Hairbrush
12. Hair things like a bobble or hairband,
    if you need them
13. Clean knickers and socks
14. Change of clothes for the next day
15. Sleepover diary and membership card

CHAPTER ONE

Greetings, earthlings! It's Rosie here – or should I say Carromi?! That's my alien name, before you think I've gone mad! Do you know how to work out your own alien name? It's dead easy.

1) Take the first three letters of your surname (mine's 'c-a-r' from Cartwright).

2) Then take the first two letters of your first name ('r-o', that's easy).

3) And finally, take the first two letters of your mum's maiden name ('m-i' for Millington in my mum's case).

4) Add them all together and there's your new name! Cool, eh?

You're probably wondering two things. Firstly, why am I wibbling on about alien names at all? And secondly, you might be thinking – hang on, *Rosie* doesn't often tell the Sleepover stories! Why's she doing this one?

Well, this is why. The story I'm about to tell is so weird and spooky and freaky that Frankie said no-one would believe her if *she* told it. Everyone would just think, "Yeah, yeah, Frankie and her vivid imagination!" But if I, Rosie the hard-boiled cynic, tell you what happened to us, you might just believe it. So here I am!

So why am I going on about alien names? Well, we've all been getting *reeeeeally* into aliens and UFOs and space and spooky things, lately, ever since Frankie first got the telescope, and...

WHOOPS! You can tell I'm not used to doing this, can't you? I haven't even told you who Frankie is, or even mentioned any of the others yet! Sorry – shall I start again?

I'm Rosie Maria Cartwright and I'm in the Sleepover Club. Do you know the others? I'll never forget the day I met them. My family had just moved to Cuddington and I had to start at Cuddington Primary School without knowing a single person. Have you ever had to start a new school where everyone knows everyone else already, and they all have their own special groups of friends? It was *soooo* horrible. I felt dead lonely and missed all my old mates like mad – until Lyndz took me under her wing, that is.

That's Lyndz for you – she's the kindest person I've ever met. Her alien name is Collyle and she'd come from Planet Nice, if she really was an alien! She'd do anything for anyone, I reckon. Well, she came right up to me in the playground and asked me if I wanted to join in with a skipping game. Then later on she told me all about this Sleepover Club she was in and asked me to join that, too. So I did!

I think the other Sleepover Clubbers were a teensy weensy bit narked about that, actually. They've all known each other since they were babies, practically, and I could tell Frankie and Kenny were sussing me out at first – trying to decide if I was good enough for their club! They must have thought so, luckily, 'cos I've been best mates with all of them ever since. Now I'm just *soooo* glad we moved to Cuddington, as I've got the most excellent friends a girl could ever wish for!

There's three others in our club, apart from Lyndz and me. For starters, there's Frankie Thomas, the crazy one who comes out with these off-the-wall ideas all the time. Planet Bonkers, that's where Frankie – or Thofral – would be from. Honestly, I don't know how she thinks of all her mad plans. She's tall and skinny, very funny and quite bossy. And boy, is she LOUD!

Kenny McKenzie's the sport freak, and if she were an alien, she'd definitely be from Planet Football! Kenny (Mcklali – her real name's Laura) is a bit wild, too. She'd do anything for a dare. Last week, she jumped off Frankie's back wall, which is about ten feet high, just because Frankie bet her 50p she couldn't do it. You can't say things like that to Kenny without her trying to prove you wrong! I couldn't watch as she did it 'cos I was convinced she'd crack her head open or break her leg or something but – whoosh! Down she jumped, cool as anything. Dusted off her shorts – and then went straight into loads of handsprings and cartwheels around the garden. "Show off," Frankie muttered in disgust, as she reached for her purse. "Makes me feel sick just looking at her!"

And last but not least there's Felicity Proudlove, who's from Planet Girly, I reckon. Her alien name should be Prfegr by rights, but as that's far too unpronounceable, we cheated a bit! Fliss's name *used* to be Sidebotham – which, as you can imagine, she hated 'cos all the boys at school called her nicknames. Then her mum remarried last month so Fliss got a new surname – Proudlove, which is almost as bad!

Anyway, just to avoid a total tongue-twister, we decided to bend the rules and use her old surname for her alien name. So now it's Sidfegr, or Sid for short! Don't ask me why, but Fliss is just totally into clothes and make-up and boys and all sorts of boring things like that. She's the only one of the Sleepover Club who'd ever *dream* of kissing pictures of boy bands in magazines, put it like that! I thought

Fliss was a bit prim and proper when I first met her, but now I've sussed she's excellent value for teasing big-time. She's like one of those clockwork toys – wind her up and watch her go! She falls for a trick every time. Me and Kenny tease her a lot – it's one of my favourite sports!

Anyway, like I said, we're the Sleepover Club, and as well as seeing each other every day at school, we also have sleepovers every Friday or Saturday at someone's house. Sometimes they're for a specific reason, like if we're planning something special together for a school project or for Brownies. But most of the time, we just play stupid games, muck about, dress up, eat loads of sweets and stay up all night whispering ghost stories. It's *sooo* much fun! Weekends are just the best. No school – and it's Sleepover time!!

Right, I think I've told you all the important bits now. On with the story!

It all started in the school holidays. August! I love that month! It was a really hot, hot, *hot* week, so Frankie suggested an outdoor sleepover at hers for that Friday.

"We can all sleep out in the garden!" she said excitedly. "We can either put up a couple of tents or just sleep in our sleeping bags under the stars!"

"Cool!" we all said, eyes lighting up at the thought. Well – nearly all of us...

"What about insects?" Fliss said at once, looking anxious.

"Well, what about them?" Kenny asked, even though we all knew what was coming.

"They'll crawl on us!" Fliss said, as if we were completely stupid. "They'll crawl on us when we're asleep – they might even crawl into our *mouths*!"

If there's one thing Fliss hates more than the sight of blood, it's creepy-crawlies. They totally freak her out!

"I've never seen that many insects in Frankie's garden," Lyndz said encouragingly. "Anyway, don't *they* sleep at night, too?"

"Oh, no – they love night time," Kenny teased. "They go berserk at night time, crawling and squirming everywhere. And they just *love* crawling into people's mouths – it's their favourite thing. If there's a mouth anywhere around, they'll all be flocking towards it, fast as you like. Queuing up for it, I'm telling you! Straight up!"

"Straight *in*, you mean!" I said. "Yum, yum, delicious!"

Fliss looked as if she was about to cry. "I know you're just trying to scare me," she said. "But now I really *really* don't want to sleep outside!"

"You're not frightened of a few teeny tiny little insects are you, Fliss?" Kenny said. "They can't hurt you!"

"Some of them can," she said defensively. "Some of them bite you. Some of them sting!" Then a look of panic spread over her face. "And what if there are snakes about? A poisonous snake can *kill* you!"

"Oh, snakes are lovely!" Lyndz – or Pet Rescue, as we sometimes call her – said. "But don't worry, there aren't any poisonous ones in this country. Apart from adders, of course."

"One might slither over you," I pointed out cheerfully.

"Or a moth might land on your face like this," Kenny said, tickling Fliss's cheek with a piece of grass.

Fliss batted it away, looking pea-green. "No, I mean it, I can't do it," she said. "I can't sleep outside – it's just too dangerous."

We all burst out laughing.

"Oh, we'll put up a tent for you, then, Indiana Jones," Frankie said. "And if you're still scared, you can sleep in the shed!"

The rest of us were all dead excited about sleeping outside. I crossed my fingers for the whole week, hoping it wouldn't rain. Frankie's garden is huge, much better than ours.

I hate our garden. When my dad moved out, he left our house and garden in a right state. I mean, it was such a *dump*, I was too embarrassed to ask anyone round for ages and ages. He keeps promising to come round and finish doing it up for us and Mum, but now he's got this new girlfriend, he always has a convenient excuse lined up to get out of it. Me and Tiffany, my big sister, have tried doing stuff in the garden to make it a bit nicer – like mowing the lawn and planting some flowers

15

here and there – but it still looks scruffy and boring.

Not like Frankie's. Her mum and dad are quite well-off and her mum loves gardening. Now Frankie's got a baby sister, Izzy, her mum has her hands full but the garden still looks great – in fact, the whole house still looks dead tidy. Still, I suppose it would if you can afford a gardener and a cleaner one day a week...

Anyway, it finally came round to Friday, and I biked over to Frankie's that afternoon. The others were already there, and I could tell when Frankie opened the front door that she was excited about something or other.

"Brilliant! Excellent! You're here," she said breathlessly. "Now I can tell everyone my big surprise!"

"Oh, no," Fliss groaned. "I don't know if I want to hear this!"

"You do," Frankie said. "You all do. I'm proud to announce that tonight, we're having a star-spotting sleepover!"

I blinked. Star-spotting?

"Really?" Fliss said excitedly. "Which stars? Oh, I wish you'd said before! I could have brought my autograph book!"

The look on Frankie's face was so disbelieving, I couldn't help a gurgle of laughter. Then Lyndz started giggling... and that was it! We all were just *roaring* with laughter – except Fliss of course.

"What?" she asked. "What's so funny?!"

"Stars in the SKY, Fliss – not famous people!" Frankie spluttered.

"Oh," said Fliss, going red.

"Yeah, 'cos there are *sooooo* many celebrities wandering around Cuddington, aren't there?" Kenny said sarcastically. "I saw Steps practising dance routines in the park yesterday, and Konnie from *Blue Peter* in the newsagent..."

"All right, all right!" Fliss said, huffily. "It was an easy mistake to make!"

"Anyway, look at this!" Frankie said, changing the subject. "Ta-da!"

She held up a large, heavy-looking black case and then opened it up. "It's a telescope!" she said, her eyes gleaming with excitement. "Mad Uncle Colin gave it me for a birthday present."

"Er… your birthday's in April," I pointed out.

"Yeah, a *late* birthday present," Frankie said. "He picked it up in an antique shop and thought I'd like it." She was fiddling around, putting it together. "Honestly, you can see the stars dead clearly. It's *wicked*!"

Fliss was wrinkling her nose. "And that's what you want us to do tonight – look at stars?" she said. "Doesn't sound much fun to me."

"Yeah, if only the telescope stretched all the way to Hollywood, eh, Fliss," Kenny said cuttingly. "Might be able to see a few *real* stars there!"

Fliss was about to pout but changed her mind and threw a cushion at Kenny instead.

"OK, funny bunny," she said. "Ha ha ha, let's all laugh at Fliss, shall we?"

"Yeah, let's," agreed Kenny. "There's always something to laugh at!"

"OK, you two, cut it out," Lyndz said.

"Yeah, 'cos I haven't even got to the best bit yet," Frankie said dramatically. "Because I've been thinking. With this telescope, we won't just be able to see loads of stars tonight – we might even be able to see UFOs!"

"UF-what?" Fliss asked.

"UFOs – you know, unidentified flying objects!" Frankie said.

Fliss was still looking blank.

Frankie sighed and rolled her eyes. "Aliens, Fliss!" she said. "Aliens!"

CHAPTER TWO

It was me who got the giggles first again. I couldn't help it! Frankie just cracks me up with her stoopid ideas. "Aliens?" I said. "Yeah, right! Little green men, eh, Frank?"

Frankie shrugged. "Why not?" she said. "Don't you watch *The X-Files*?"

"Yeah!" I said. "And that's a TV programme. It's not real, you know!"

"My gran saw a ghost once," Lyndz put in helpfully.

"Ghosts are ghosts," Kenny said. "Frankie's talking about extra-terrestrials. Aliens from another world who can suck out your brain with a single *slurp*..."

"Stop it, Kenny," Fliss ordered. "I know you're trying to spook me again. Well, it won't work!"

"There is a lot of evidence that aliens exist…" Frankie started bossily.

I wasn't having any of that! "A lot of hoaxes, you mean!" I said. "Nothing has ever been proved, Frankie – except that some people have a very vivid imagination!"

Frankie was just about to reply when her mum shouted to us all: "Girls! Tea's ready!"

"Saved by the parent," Frankie muttered, as we went into the kitchen.

But if I thought that was going to be the end of the alien theme, I was wrong! Frankie had been busy all morning making – no, not fairy cakes – *alien* cakes, which were bright green with funny face decorations. Then her mum had continued the idea for the rest of the meal. The egg sandwiches had an extra ingredient of food colouring to make them green, pink and blue, and there was a red jelly that Frankie had mashed up into red, wobbling lumps. "Alien-brain jelly," she proudly informed us.

I saw Fliss look anxiously around the table

for anything vaguely normal, but everything had had the extra-terrestrial treatment. I'll say one thing for Frankie – she doesn't do things by halves! We even had lime cordial – I mean "alien blood" – to drink.

"Right, let's set up the telescope," Frankie said as soon as we finished.

"But it's still light," Kenny pointed out. It wasn't even seven o'clock, right in the middle of summer!

"Do we have to?" moaned Fliss. "Can't we play a game?"

Even Frankie's mum agreed. "You won't be able to see anything yet," she said, clearing the plates away.

Frankie hates having to wait for anything. "OK – why don't we watch a spooky film, to get us in the mood, then?" she said.

"What, *ET*?" I scoffed. "Yeah, that's really scary!"

Kenny looked longingly outside. She hates being cooped up indoors. She's only happy when she's racing about, using up tons of energy, I think. "Why don't we set up camp in the garden?" she said.

Frankie was starting to get a bit rattled. "Not *ET*! And we can sort the camp out later, Kenz," she said. "No, I was thinking of *The X-Files* – you know, the one that was on really late in the week? Mum taped it for me. What do you reckon?"

"As long as *everyone* wants to," Mrs Thomas interrupted. "I don't want anyone to get nightmares tonight."

"Oh, Mum!" Frankie begged. "Go on, please – none of us *ever* gets nightmares, I swear!"

Fliss bit her lip at that point. She gets terrible nightmares sometimes if we've all been telling ghost stories.

Just at that moment, baby Izzy burst into howls.

"Well..." Frankie's mum said, still not totally convinced, but too concerned about Izzy to argue any more. "OK, then."

"Yay!" shouted Frankie, jumping up and down.

"As long as you promise me that if anyone gets too scared, you'll stop the tape, OK?" she said, hurrying out of the room with Izzy.

Frankie winked at us. "Izzy is *soooo* cool!

She's got the knack of crying just when Mum's about to stop me doing something!" she said happily. "Come on – let's watch some *X-Files* action on the box!"

It was a brilliant programme – even if we were hiding behind cushions for a lot of it! I don't think Fliss saw more than ten minutes of it, as she refused point-blank to watch any of the scary bits.

Then, by the time it had finished, it was finally getting dark. Frankie was *soooo* excited. You'd think she'd never seen darkness before!

We went out into the garden to set up camp. It was such a hot evening that me, Kenny, Frankie and Lyndz all wanted to sleep under the stars in our sleeping bags. Fliss was still determined not to, so Frankie threw an old sheet over the washing line and pegged the corners into the ground.

"Da-da! Easiest tent in the world or what?!" she said.

Fliss's face fell. "But snakes can still crawl in through the ends," she pointed out, looking very doubtful about the "easiest tent in the world".

Frankie thought quickly. "But if there are any snakes around, they'll go straight to the pond over there," she said. "Snakes love swimming at night, don't they, Lyndz?"

I could tell Frankie was fibbing and knew nothing whatsoever about snakes' night habits – but Fliss seemed to want to believe it.

"Er, yeah, I think so," Lyndz said, sounding doubtful.

"There you go then!" Frankie said. "They won't bother coming near you when the pond's right over there! Problem solved!"

We all helped set up the telescope. There seemed to be lots of fiddly bits to it, what with all the lenses and the stand and everything.

"Hey, why don't we spy into your neighbours' houses?" Kenny suggested, once it was all set up. "That would be so cool! We could see everything they were up to!"

"Not half as cool as seeing an alien," Frankie said, her eye glued to the end of the telescope. "Right – I've got it lined up to see the Plough – anyone want to have a look?"

"The Plough?" Lyndz asked.

"It's a constellation," Frankie said

importantly. "It's meant to look like the shape of a plough, but if you ask me, it's more like a saucepan."

I had a look, then Lyndz, then Kenny. I couldn't really see the plough-shape myself, but it was quite cool seeing the stars so much clearer.

"Fliss, do you want a look?" Frankie asked.

There was a moment's silence – and we all turned round to look at Fliss, who was reading something in a book with her torch. She looked up. "What did you say?" she asked.

"What's that – *My Big Book of Insects*?" Kenny said, trying to read the cover. "*The Alien-Spotter's Guide to Mars*?"

Fliss held it up so we could see. *Virgo – Your Daily Stars in 2000*, it was called. "It's my horoscopes book," she said solemnly. "I got it half-price in a sale. Good eh?"

"Half-price?" I snorted. "I'm not surprised – over half the year's gone already!"

"Yeah, but I've read my horoscopes for all the days that have already gone as well," she said defensively.

"Well, what's the point of that?" Kenny

asked. She's as cynical as me when it comes to airy-fairy things like horoscopes. What a load of old rubbish!

Fliss gave this knowing sort of smile. "Well, the point is, Kenny, that everything in here has come true!" she said. "Take last month – Rosie's birthday."

"What, your horoscopes book knew it was my birthday?" I said sarcastically. "Let's have a look!"

I grabbed it off her and read the entry for my birthday, July 15th. "'A good day for being with friends and family'," I read aloud. "'There may be something to celebrate.'" I passed the book back to her. "Big deal!" I said. "You see your family every day anyway – and you see us most days, too. So what?"

"'Something to celebrate' – that was your birthday," Fliss persisted. "And I spent the day with friends – we all went to the park, didn't we? See! It's all true!"

I caught Kenny's eye, and we both shook our heads, grinning. Fliss is just *soooo* gullible! She's a sucker for anything like that.

"So what are your stars for today?" Lyndz

asked quickly before either of us could make any more horrible remarks.

"Well, that's what I was just reading," Fliss said. "It's quite an exciting one today. 'Watch out for something unexpected. A new cycle begins today, and seeing is definitely believing'." She closed the book with a snap. "Sounds good, eh?"

"'A new cycle' – does that mean your step-dad's fixed your bike?" Kenny said.

"'Something unexpected' – that probably means a moth flying into your mouth," I teased. "Doesn't sound much fun to me!"

I could tell Frankie was getting bored of this conversation. "That's enough about your stars, Fliss," she said. "Let's get back to the REAL stars again! Do you want a look?"

"Watch out for something unexpected, remember!" Kenny teased as Fliss put her book down. "Something totally unexpected – like the moon!"

"Shut up, Kenny!" Fliss said, sticking her nose in the air.

"Oh, ignore her," Lyndz said. "She's just jealous of your exciting horoscope, Fliss!"

"Mmm, yeah, absolutely," Kenny said, sticking her tongue out. "Ooh, I'm *soooo* jealous!"

Fliss put one eye to the telescope and shut the other. Her hands came around the telescope to hold it steady. "Wow!" she said. "Stars!"

Then she looked over at Kenny triumphantly. "See? That was unexpected. I had no idea I was going to be looking through a telescope today – the book was right!"

Kenny threw a jelly baby at Fliss, which bounced straight off her head. "And *that* was something *else* unexpected!" she said. "Now all you need is to get your bike fixed and the whole horoscope will be right!"

"Oh shut up!" Fliss said crossly, and swung the telescope round so it was pointing at Kenny. Then she giggled. "Eurgh, Kenny, I can see right up your nose!" she said. "And I think you've got a spot coming on your forehead!"

"Don't swing it around like that, Fliss!" Frankie said sternly. "It's meant to point up at the sky! Why do you want to look even closer at Kenny's ugly mug, anyway?"

"Sorry, Frankie," Fliss said, and started moving the telescope back up towards the stars again. Then she stopped and peered through the lens, frowning at something. "What on earth is THAT?" she muttered to herself. "There aren't any *green* stars, are there?"

We all looked at each other. What was Fliss on about now?

"Ooh, it's moving up and down now," she said excitedly. "Frankie – quick, come and look at this!"

Frankie was over in a shot, and grabbed the telescope off her.

"I don't believe it!" she murmured, peering through. "I just don't believe it! There really is something there! Green flashing lights – moving up and down!" She stood back and looked at us, her mouth hanging open. "Quick, all of you, look!"

We each looked at the green lights in turn. I was the last one to look and, to be honest, I didn't think for a minute it would be anything weird. But sure enough, I did see the green lights Fliss had spotted moving slowly up in the air, and then down again. Then they vanished.

"They've gone!" I said, moving the telescope up and down, trying to spot them again. "They seemed to go down – and then just disappeared."

Frankie was practically jumping up and down in excitement. "I can't believe we've seen a spaceship!" she squeaked. "I just can't believe we saw it!"

"Now, wait a minute..." I said. No-one had said anything about a spaceship until then.

"Aliens!" Frankie said. "Here in Cuddington!" She stood and looked in the direction the telescope was pointing. "That's Cuddington Hill over there," she said. "What if aliens have landed on Cuddington Hill?!"

CHAPTER THREE

We all stared at each other in disbelief.

"*I* saw them first," Fliss said importantly – and then her eyes went wide. "See? THAT must have been what my horoscope book was talking about. Aliens! I mean, how unexpected can you get?!"

"That is completely and totally and utterly unexpected," Lyndz agreed solemnly.

There was a moment's silence while we all thought about it.

"So if aliens have landed in Cuddington," Kenny said slowly and dramatically, "how long have we got before they get off their ship and come to get us?"

We all looked at each other and screamed at the same time – even me!

"There's no way on earth I'm sleeping out here now!" Fliss said, grabbing her book and sleeping bag. "No way!"

"Nor me," said Lyndz, shuddering. "I don't want to be an alien breakfast!"

"Quick!" Frankie said. "Abandon mission – now!"

We grabbed our sleeping bags and pillows, and Frankie picked up the telescope and we ran into the house as fast as possible. Safely inside the kitchen, we all jumped around screeching hysterically. Whether it was aliens or not, SOMETHING had definitely landed on Cuddington Hill – and none of us fancied sleeping outside to find out WHAT!

Now you can say what you like about me, but one thing I'm not is superstitious. I don't really believe in any of that black cat, walking under ladders, two magpies stuff for starters – and I certainly don't believe in fairies, witches, ghosts and aliens! Yet suddenly I was feeling just as spooked as all the others. I really

REALLY didn't want to sleep in the garden, that was for sure, even though I was convinced there had to be a perfectly good explanation for seeing those green lights on Cuddington Hill. I mean, this was the twenty-first century after all!

But you know when everyone around you is getting really scared, and you've just seen a creepy TV programme, and there's a little voice in your head saying "What if...?" Well, that's what I was feeling – that delicious kind of scared, jumpy feeling in my tummy. I mean, what if we really *had* seen something weird? What then? Even though I knew deep down that aliens were just something you saw in films, the creepy feeling, plus the hysteria of all the others, was really getting to me!

Of course, Frankie's mum and dad weren't having any of it.

"I knew this would happen if you watched that programme!" Mrs Thomas said, sounding annoyed. "You watch a programme about aliens – and then you're convinced you've seen aliens in Cuddington! What a coincidence!"

Put like that, of course, it did sound a bit daft.

"I know what I saw, Mum," Frankie said defiantly. "And we ALL saw it, so there!"

Frankie's dad thought the whole thing was hilarious. "Ooh, look, girls – the TV reception has gone a bit fuzzy," he said. "Must be the alien landing interfering with transmission!"

"Da-a-a-a-ad!" Frankie said crossly. "Don't blame us if the body-snatchers come in the night, then!"

"I promise I won't blame you," he said, trying not to smile. "Now I think you five should transport yourselves to bed. And Frankie..."

"Yes, Dad?"

"Make sure your bedroom window's closed." He winked at us. "We wouldn't want anything clambering in there while you're asleep, would we?"

I laughed at that, but I thought Fliss was going to faint, she looked so white.

"Why did he have to say that?" she whispered as we were going upstairs. "I'll NEVER be able to sleep now!"

"At least there aren't any snakes or insects in Frankie's bedroom," Lyndz pointed out comfortingly.

"I think I'd rather have a few insects than green slimy aliens!" Fliss said with a shudder. "Bagsy me not sleeping by the window!"

"Turn around, touch the ground, bagsy not me!" Lyndz said quickly.

In the end we had to toss for it, because no-one really wanted to sleep by the window, not even fearless Frankie and Kenny! Frankie lost the toss – but she persuaded her mum to let Pepsi the dog sleep in there with us, just to protect us from anything scary.

It was just about impossible to get to sleep that night. Normally on sleepover nights, as you can imagine, we don't fall asleep until really really late anyway because we're always whispering silly things to each other or telling jokes, or sometimes Kenny tells one of her grisly ghost stories to scare us.

But on this particular night, every time there was the teeniest tiniest noise, Fliss sat bolt upright in the darkness and said, "What was THAT?"

"Mum and Dad in the kitchen," Frankie would say, or "A car outside," or "The wind in the trees."

Suddenly there came this low humming sound, so low you had to really strain your ears to hear it. Then it stopped.

"W-w-w-what was that?" Kenny asked. Even *she* sounded scared now.

No-one could think of anything it might have been.

"It's probably nothing," I said. I was trying to sound brave but my voice had a definite wobble to it.

Then the humming started again. Very very faint. We all lay as still as still, listening to it. There's something about the darkness that makes noises sound even scarier than usual, do you know what I mean?

"What do you think it is?" Fliss whispered.

Again it stopped.

"I think it's the spaceship hovering outside," Kenny whispered, and Fliss let out a muffled scream as she pulled her sleeping bag right over her head.

Then there was a giggle. A Kenny giggle.

"Mmmmm," she hummed loudly and giggled some more. "Got you all there, didn't I?" she laughed. "Mmmmm – quick, the spaceship's getting nearer!"

I rolled over on top of her. "You evil cow!" I said, starting to giggle myself – in sheer relief as much as anything! "Come on, you lot – pile on!"

"You mean it was you all along?!" Fliss said indignantly, poking her head out of the sleeping bag again. "Right! You're gonna pay for that, McKenzie!"

We all piled on to Kenny until she begged for mercy. "No – aaargh! Stop! Mercy! Mercy!" she squeaked breathlessly. "I'm sorry – I couldn't resist!"

We all got a bad case of the giggles after that. It was that nervous sort of giggling where you just can't stop yourself.

Then there was a tap at the door.

"Aaaargh!" we all screamed, and burst out giggling again.

"Girls, it's half past eleven," called Mr Thomas through the door. "Any more racket and I'll send the aliens in to keep you quiet!"

That just made us even worse! Trying to giggle quietly is just *soooo* difficult! I had to put some of my sleeping bag in my mouth to try and keep the volume down, but I had Lyndz clutching me, shaking with laughter on one side, and I could feel Frankie heaving with giggles on the other.

"I need some sweets to calm me down," Lyndz said weakly after a few minutes.

"Yeah, chocolate, good idea!" Kenny said. "Stuff some in your mouth and you won't be able to laugh so much!"

We all had a bit of Frankie's huge Dairy Milk bar that she'd bought, and sure enough, as the chocolate melted in our mouths, I started to feel a bit better.

"I wonder what it was we saw tonight," I said, feeling a bit sleepier. "Maybe it was just a low-flying plane."

"A low-flying plane that goes up and down with green lights on it?" Frankie snorted. "Do me a favour!"

"What do you think aliens look like?" Fliss wondered aloud.

"Probably a bit like you," Kenny said

cheekily. "A bit better-looking though, I should think..."

Whoomp! Fliss chucked her teddy bear over at Kenny. I forgot to tell you, Fliss is actually *reeeeaaaallly* pretty – but doesn't she just know it! Long blonde hair and big blue eyes, you know the sort. She's got the type of face that grannies always make comments about when they see her. "Ooh, isn't she an angel?", that sort of thing.

"Teddy fight!" said Kenny in a low voice, chucking hers at Lyndz. Soon there were teddies flying in all directions through the darkness. Pepsi got a bit excited and started barking and running around, trying to catch one in his mouth.

"Pepsi, get off!" Lyndz giggled. "Ugh, he's slobbered all over Barnaby!"

"Keep it down in there, girls!" shouted Mr Thomas again. "Last warning, Frankie!"

Once we'd all calmed down, Frankie was the first one to speak. "I know it's late now and we should get to sleep," she whispered. "But all I want to say is this. I don't know what we saw out there tonight, but I have this strange feeling that it was something really freaky that we just happened to stumble upon. Anyway, whatever it was, I know one thing for sure. Tomorrow morning we're going to go to Cuddington Hill and have a good look around. Because I for one want to get to the bottom of this!"

"Me too," said Kenny.

"Me three," said Lyndz.

"Me four," said Fliss. "But only if it's not going to be too scary," she added quickly.

There was a silence while I thought about it. Why not? I *was* starting to feel pretty curious about the whole thing myself.

"Me five," I said. "So we're all in it together!"

CHAPTER FOUR

Even though, like I told you, I don't believe in alien stuff, I found that I couldn't get to sleep that night. The little "What if...?" voice just wouldn't go away. What if we'd really stumbled upon something? We could be famous all over the world if we'd really spotted an alien spaceship. We might even get to be on telly and everything!

Then the sensible voice would start. Of course it wasn't an alien spaceship. There was no such thing! So there had to be a logical explanation. But what?

In the end, my poor brain got so exhausted from all its weird thoughts, I finally managed to get some shut-eye. But even then, my dreams were full of flashing lights and little green men – all those things I'd been so scornful about earlier! It really was a strange kind of night.

Next morning, it was still the only thing we could talk about.

"I couldn't stop dreaming about aliens last night," Lyndz said in a low voice, pouring Cheerios into a bowl at the breakfast table. "And in one dream, there was this green slimy figure that kept talking to me. Telling me to do things – and then I couldn't help doing everything it said! Spooky, eh?"

"Did it tell you to pass the milk over to me?" Kenny said, grinning. "Oh, no, I just told you that, didn't I?"

Fliss was spreading jam on her toast, and not saying much. She looked really tired – I guessed she hadn't slept very well either.

"In my dream, an alien shot straight out of your stomach, Kenz," Frankie said lightly, taking a big bite of toast. "Just like in *The X-Files*. It was gr-r-r-ross!"

Kenny looked down at her tummy. "I

thought I felt something squirming about in there," she said cheerfully, and gave it a pat. "I thought it was just my Rice Krispies snapping, crackling and popping away!"

Fliss pulled a sick face. "Kenny, do you have to?" she said. "I don't want to think about an alien coming out of you – not when you're sitting right next to me, anyway!"

"I wonder if THAT's in your horoscope book?" Kenny teased. "'Today you will be shocked by an alien's head emerging from your friend's stomach...' Now if your book said that, it WOULD impress me!"

"So is everyone still up for going over to Cuddington Hill today?" I asked as Fliss picked up her horoscope book to check her stars. "Not that I believe for a minute that there's any alien goings-on, of course – but it would be good just to check that there's nothing freaky up there."

"And it would be even better to see that there IS something freaky up there!" Frankie said happily. "Watch out, you extra-terrestrials – the Sleepover Club is coming to check you out!"

44

"I wonder if the aliens are friendly?" Lyndz pondered.

"Oh, I doubt it," Kenny said. "Probably the head-tearing-off type. Did you see that film where—"

"Uh-oh," Fliss said loudly. She put her book down, looking worried. "My stars say that I'm to 'tread carefully' today. Do you think that means we shouldn't go up to the hill?"

"Not on your nelly!" Frankie said. "Wild horses couldn't keep me away!"

"What about wild aliens?" I asked with a giggle.

"The wilder the better!" Kenny said. "Come on – eat up, everyone! I want my first ride in a spaceship and I want it now!"

Luckily we all had our bikes with us, which made it a lot easier to get to Cuddington Hill. Frankie and Kenny raced ahead as usual, both wanting to get there first. Me, Lyndz and Fliss went along slower behind them.

Both Frankie and Kenny have got really flash mountain bikes with loads of gears, whereas me and Lyndz have got old hand-me-down cronks that my older sister and her older brothers had before us. So once those two get going, we haven't got a chance of keeping up.

Fliss's bike is pretty nice, too, but she doesn't like going very fast – one, because she hates getting her hair blown about too much, and two, because she says high speeds make her feel sick. But then again, EVERYTHING makes Fliss feel sick, so that's not really surprising!

As soon as Kenny and Frankie were out of sight, Fliss put her brakes on and stopped.

"What's up?" I called over my shoulder. I thought she must have a puncture or something. Me and Lyndz walked our bikes back to her.

"Is your bike OK?" Lyndz asked.

"It's not my bike – it's this whole thing about looking for aliens," Fliss said, looking anxious. "Do you really think it's such a good idea? I can't help thinking about what my horoscopes book warned…"

"Oh, stuff your horoscopes book!" I said. "C'mon, Fliss – one for all and all for one, eh?

Anyway, if you ask me, this whole alien thing is a load of rubbish. There's no such thing! We'll get to Cuddington Hill and you and me can have a good old laugh at Frankie for believing in such nonsense. How about that?"

She still didn't look convinced.

"Come on, Fliss," Lyndz said. "Rosie's right. It's probably nothing. Just think how much better you're going to feel when we find nothing there."

"No more awful scary dreams," I said encouragingly. "Think about it!"

I could see she liked the sound of that idea.

"OK," she said finally, throwing a leg over her bike again. "Let's do it. Let's prove the 'no-alien' theory!"

So off we went again. It was an absolute stonker of a day – bright blue sky and not even a *wisp* of cloud around. It was gorgeous to get a breeze blowing through my hair. Every time we went down a hill, I took my feet off the pedals and stuck them out to the sides. *Wheeeeee!*

We met Frankie and Kenny at the park gates.

"About time!" Frankie said.

I could see Fliss's face turning a bit pink.

"Sorry, Fliss thought she had a puncture but it was OK after all," I said quickly, and she shot me a grateful look. See! I'm not horrible to our Sidfegr ALL the time!!

We pushed our bikes up to the top of Cuddington Hill. It's such a steep hill, not even Kenny fancied her chances cycling up it! "If it was cold, I would," she said, as we puffed our way up the hill. "But as it's so boilingly hot today – no chance!"

"Have you noticed how there's not many people around?" Frankie said. "I wonder if the aliens have been kidnapping a few?"

"Well, it IS nearly lunchtime, I suppose..." Kenny said. "They're probably a bit on the peckish side."

I rolled my eyes. "You two! You're going to be *soooo* disappointed when you realise that actually there were no aliens in Cuddington last night!"

"And YOU are going to be even more disappointed when an alien gobbles you up for being a non-believer!" Frankie retorted.

"Yeah, while me and Frank are worshipped

and crowned queens among the aliens because we believed in them all along!" Kenny said, sticking her tongue out.

I opened my mouth to reply – but just then there was an unmistakable *squelch*!

I turned round to see where it had come from.

Uh-oh...

"Oh, NO!" groaned Fliss. "My new Nikes! Look at them!"

We all just fell about laughing to see that Fliss had trodden straight in a pile of horse poo. It was all over her gleaming white trainers and her face was an absolute picture.

"Trust you, big-foot!" Frankie giggled. "I think your feet have got a poo-magnet on them – you're ALWAYS treading in it!"

"Why do they let horses in this park anyway?" Fliss was fuming. "Nasty great things, pooing everywhere! Ugh! And it STINKS!!"

I had to put my bike down and roll on the grass, I was so helpless with laughter. "Oh, Fliss," I gurgled, "your horoscope DID tell you to 'tread carefully', didn't it?!"

Fliss glared at me as she tried to scrape it off on to the path. "Ugh! Stupid horses!"

"Horses can't help it if they want to poo!" Lyndz said hotly. She's a mad keen rider, so doesn't like ANY criticism of her favourite animal! "You should look where you're going!"

"Good old Fliss," Kenny chortled merrily. "We can always count on you to tread carefully, can't we?"

"Oh, button it, Kenny!" Fliss snapped. "I wish we'd never come on this *stooo*pid bike ride in the first place!"

We carried on up the hill. Fliss was in a total strop, and the rest of us kept bursting into giggles every time we saw her indignant face. Fliss has one of the most expressive faces I've ever seen – and when she's in a bad mood, the whole world knows about it!

We carried on in silence until we got to the top. It was so steep, I could hardly speak with all my huffing and puffing!

Kenny, of course, still had bags of energy. She started running with her bike, then dumped it on the ground once she'd reached the top of the hill. "Come on, you lot!" she yelled, then ran off ahead to look for clues.

We trudged along behind – and then Kenny gave an excited shout. "Quick! Come and look at this!"

CHAPTER FIVE

Suddenly, my legs didn't feel quite so tired any more. We all dropped our bikes in a heap and chased up the rest of the hill to see what she'd found.

"Look! Look! Scorch marks on the grass!" she was yelling. "This must be where the spaceship landed!"

We all knelt on the grass to look closer. Sure enough, there were three or four marks, about thirty centimetres long, where the grass was brown and burned.

"This is proof," Frankie said excitedly. "I've never seen anything like it! This is definite proof!"

She took out her camera and started taking lots of pictures of the scorched grass. "Even *you've* got to admit that this is proof, Rosie!"

I shook my head. "Sorry, Frank. Anything could have scorched that grass," I said. "Doesn't mean it's a spaceship. Anyway – those marks aren't very long, are they? Are you telling me that the spaceship was that small?"

"The scorch marks could be from its feet as it landed," Lyndz pointed out. "Or from some sort of exhaust pipe, you know, like on cars? They always get really hot, don't they?"

She was sounding just as excited as Frankie and Kenny.

"And the aliens might shrink themselves to travel around, anyway," Frankie said. "Travel light, that's what my gran always says!"

I still wasn't convinced one bit!

"There's nothing about those marks that says 'spaceship' to me," I said. I was actually feeling the teensiest bit disappointed, I've got to admit. "What do you reckon, Fliss?"

Fliss's eyes were wide and frightened. "You said there'd be nothing up here, Rosie – and there is!" she said. She sounded quite accusing. She'd obviously really been wanting NOT to have to believe in the spaceship idea. "You can't prove there was nothing there last night now, can you?"

I shrugged impatiently. "This is plain daft!" I said. "A few scorch marks on the grass and you're all freaking out on me! Give me some more proof then – I bet you any money you can't!"

Frankie was scrabbling on the ground. "Oh no?" she said triumphantly. "What's THIS, then?"

We all went over to have a look. In Frankie's hand there was a small, round, flat disc. It looked a bit like a tiddlywink, but it was a bright, shimmering green colour.

"Cool or what?" Frankie said as we all stared at it.

Fliss looked she was going to cry. "I've NEVER seen anything like that before," she said. "Rosie – quick, tell me what it is!"

I grabbed it out of Frankie's hand and peered at it.

"I'm not sure," I said slowly, turning it over

in my hand. "It looks like something out of a board game."

"Oh, yeah, so who's going to come up to the top of Cuddington Hill and play a board game – oh, and at the same time, scorch the grass a few times?" Kenny said ultra-sarcastically. "Hmmm... how about no-one?!"

To be honest, I was totally baffled. I was racking my brain trying to think of a logical explanation but nothing was coming. "Er..." I said, lamely.

"Maybe it's an alien coin," Lyndz said breathlessly. "Maybe one of them dropped it by mistake."

"Wicked! I wonder what we could buy with this?" Frankie said, grabbing it back from me. "A laser gun, maybe, or even a return trip to Mars!"

"I don't like this," Fliss muttered. "I don't like this one bit! I KNEW we shouldn't have come up here. First I tread in horse muck, and then we find an alien coin."

Then a thought struck her, and she looked even more upset. "And what if the aliens want it BACK? What if they come to find us so they

can take it back? And it might not be a coin –
it might be a... a baby alien, for all we know!"

Fliss was gibbering like a maniac, but
Frankie and Kenny just seemed even more
excited by the idea.

"I'll look after it!" Kenny said at once, her
hand shooting out to snatch the disc.

"No, you will not!" Frankie said immediately,
shoving the disc in her pocket. "Finders
keepers, losers weepers – so there!"

"Frankie, are you sure you want to look after
it?" Lyndz said, sounding nervous. "What if
Fliss is right – what if an alien comes to take it
back?"

"Then I will be the happiest girl in
Cuddington!" Frankie said, grinning. "In fact,
I'm really REEEEALLY hoping an alien DOES
come to take it back. It would be awesome!
Can you imagine?!"

"Can I have another look at it?" I asked. By
now, I was desperate to be able to prove it was
nothing extra-terrestrial. I just couldn't go
along with this alien thing like the others –
there *had* to be an explanation to it all.

I peered at the disc again. It was very light in

my hand – I wasn't sure if it was made of metal or what. It had a slight metallic sheen to it, but felt very warm on my skin, not cold like normal metals.

I handed it back, pulling a face. "I'm totally in the dark," I admitted. "I'm sure it's nothing to do with a spaceship, but..."

"So what is it, then, smarty-pants?" crowed Kenny.

I shook my head. "That's the problem," I said. "I just don't know!"

We hunted around for a while longer to see if there were any more clues, but no-one could find anything. I was quite relieved, to be honest. My brain had quite enough to be working on as it was!

When it got to about midday, it was starting to feel really hot on top of the hill.

"Anyone fancy going for a swim this afternoon?" Kenny said, blowing her fringe out of her eyes.

"Yes!" Fliss said at once. "Let's get away from this spooky place – it's giving me the creeps."

"Hold your horses," Frankie said. "I think we should make notes of all our evidence first."

She held up a notebook. "This was going to be a star-spotting notebook, but I think it's going to have to be an alien-spotting book now!"

"Coo-*ell*!" Kenny said. "What are you going to put in it?"

"Well, while we're up here, I'm going to sketch a picture of these scorch marks," she said, turning to the first page.

I pulled a face. "That'll be an interesting picture!" I said sarcastically.

"It's the sort of thing Sherlock Holmes would do," Lyndz said. "You never know, it might jog our memories later on."

"And when I get my film developed, we can stick the pictures in, too," Frankie said. "Now, how long would you say that mark was?"

While the others discussed the marks, I stared into space, thinking how hot it was. And then I saw two girls, about our age, one tall and thin, one small and chubby, coming up the hill towards us, looking very hot and bothered as they made the last steep climb.

"Look! It's the M&Ms!" I said to the others. "What do you think they're doing here?"

In case you didn't know, the M&Ms are Emily Berryman and Emma Hughes – our biggest enemies at school. They are the most absolutely vile, hideous, yucky people in the world, and we always seem to be getting into trouble with them. Luckily, both Ms are a bit dim so we can usually get one over on them, but it has been known for them to trick *us* just as horribly at times!

"Quick, hide the book!" Kenny told Frankie. "We don't want them knowing what we're up to."

"Yeah, no-one say a word about it," Frankie said, stuffing the notebook into her pocket. "Here they come!"

Out of the corner of my eye, I just happened to catch sight of my water bottle on my bike. It's one of those ones with a built-in straw so you can drink while you cycle. Hmm! I thought. Maybe if....

I pulled it off the front of my bike and showed Kenny. "What do you reckon? Super-squirter water pistol or what?"

"I like it!" Kenny said, grabbing hers. "Anyone else got one? Those two look as if they need cooling down a bit!"

From where we were, right on top of the hill, we were in a brilliant spot to get the M&Ms. As soon as they rounded the corner and came into view, Frankie shouted, "Aim... fire!" and all five of us squirted our water bottles at them, *right* into their faces!

I've never seen anyone look more shocked in their lives! Emily and Emma both squealed as they got hit by five streams of water. Within seconds they were totally drenched!

"I might have known it was you lot!" Emily raged. "Look what you've done to my hair! I've just come back from the hairdressers, you know!"

We all burst into giggles at their angry faces and flattened hair.

"I think the 'wet look' looks even better on you!" spluttered Kenny. "Anyway, must dash – things to do, you know..."

We picked up our bikes and raced off down the hill again, away from the furious Ms. They were still so puffed out from climbing the hill that they didn't even have the energy to chase after us.

"Nice work, team," Kenny chuckled as we skidded all the way down. "Did you see their faces? Did we surprise them or WHAT?!"

At the bottom of the hill, we collapsed in a heap of giggles.

"They looked *soooo* mad!" Lyndz spluttered. "They're really going to be out to get us back now!"

"Oh, tremble, tremble!" I said. "Because they're so scary – not!"

"That was fun, wasn't it?" Fliss said happily. "Apart from my trainers getting ruined, of course. Did you finish writing everything up, Frankie?"

"Just about," Frankie said. "What a great day this is turning out to be! Finding clues to an alien landing *and* winding up the M&Ms!"

"Well, we still haven't really proved anything about this so-called alien landing," I said cautiously.

"We've proved that we've got to check THIS out further," Frankie said, still fiddling with the green disc. "And we've proved that, for the

61

first time, the Sleepover Club are stumped! And I HATE being stumped!"

"We definitely need to keep an eye on this hill," Lyndz agreed. "Maybe we'll see the spaceship again – and you never know, next time, we might find something else that even *Rosie* believes in!"

"Next sleepover, we'll definitely have to have another star-spotting session," Frankie said. "It's a date!"

CHAPTER SIX

The next week was the last week of the school holidays. BOOO! Why do the summer holidays whizz by *soooo* quickly? One minute you've got weeks and weeks of no school stretching ahead of you – and the next minute, boom! It's all over and you've got to get your school uniform on again. Gutted!

The last week of the holidays went by quickest of all, of course, and I hardly got a chance to see the others. I went down to the river a couple of times with my brother Adam, who loves fishing.

I don't know if any of the others have told you, but Adam's in a wheelchair 'cos he's got cerebral palsy. That means he can't walk and he can't talk very well either, although he's got this computerised voice box which makes him sound a bit like something out of Star Wars, if you ask me. He can do a wicked Darth Vader impression without even trying!

Some people feel sorry for my brother when they see him and he gets a bit sick of that. I don't feel sorry for him one bit, because most of the time, he's trying to wind me up. He's all right really, though – for a boy!

The rest of the week was dead busy – seeing Dad and Granny and Grandpa, going shopping with my mum for new school shoes... you know what it can be like. It felt like I was in a bit of a whirl with all the family stuff and getting ready for school again. So I was *reeeally* glad when it was finally Friday and we could have another sleepover at Frankie's!

It was actually Kenny's turn to have the sleepover but Frankie got all bossy about her telescope and said she didn't want to have to drag it round to anyone else's house. I reckon that was just an excuse to have the sleepover at hers again!

Kenny didn't mind though – it can be a bit of a nightmare staying at her house 'cos her horrible sister Molly always tries to wreck our sleepovers. So Frankie's it was, then!

This time, there was no waiting till it got dark. By the time the rest of us got round there, around four that afternoon, Frankie had already set up the telescope – or 'Mission Control' as she insisted on calling it! – in the back garden. She had also set up a little camping table and chair by the telescope, complete with paper and different coloured pens.

"Well, like my gran says, if you're going to do something, you may as well do it right!" she said importantly.

Fliss waved her horoscope book in the air. "I have a feeling something may happen again tonight," she said mysteriously. "My horoscope for today says, 'the plot thickens' – I'm sure that means we'll see those lights again!"

"Or even be visited by the aliens, trying to get their coin back," Kenny said, with a wicked grin.

Frankie looked disappointed. "All week I've been hoping they would come for it," she said. "And there's absolutely nothing! Not even one little teeny tiny alien landing on Melford Road! So unfair!"

"Ooh, they're just *sooo* unreliable, aren't they?" I said sarcastically. "So what shall we play while we wait for it to get dark?"

"How about Alien Footsteps?" said Kenny. "It's a bit like Grandmother's Footsteps – but the grandmother is an alien!"

I could see there was going to be NO let-up from aliens that night! Even Fliss seemed to be well into the idea now – especially since her horoscope book was predicting further action!

Once we'd had a few energetic rounds of Alien Footsteps – where Kenny insisted on being the alien that chased the loser (Frankie) round the garden – Fliss pulled a box out of her sleepover bag.

"You're not the only one to get a birthday present this month, Frankie," she said. "Look at this!"

"Your birthday's NEXT month," Lyndz said. "How come you opened it early?"

Fliss looked a bit sheepish. "Well, at home, they've all been calling me Mystic Flisstic, 'cos of my horoscope book," she said, "and—"

"Mystic Flisstic! I like it!" Kenny laughed. "I'm afraid that is your new nickname with us too now, Mystic!"

"Yeah, yeah," said Fliss, tossing her hair. She'd obviously been hearing that nickname a LOT! "Well, anyway, Andy found this in Cuddington Market and said I ought to have it early, so I could use it tonight. 'Cos I've told them all about the aliens, you see, and…"

"So what is it?" Frankie said impatiently. "The suspense is killing us, Flisstic!"

Fliss pulled out a black plastic ball, about the size of a grapefruit, and held it up in the air dramatically. "This is the Magic-8 ball," she said solemnly.

"Ace, can we use it for a football?" Kenny asked.

"Don't you dare!" Fliss cried, clutching it to her chest protectively.

"Didn't Bart have one of those on *The Simpsons*?" I asked. I was sure I'd seen one before.

"Yes! The fortune-telling ball!" Lyndz said. "I've seen that one!"

"Is that what it is, Fliss?" Frankie asked. "Does it tell your fortune?"

"Well, sort of," Fliss said. "You have to ask it a question. Then I turn it upside down and the answer pops up."

"What's the capital of China?" Kenny asked the ball at once. "Who's the manager of Leicester City football club? And what's my middle name?"

"It doesn't answer *that* sort of question!" Lyndz said.

"How convenient!" I muttered under my breath.

"It's yes-no questions only," Fliss said. "Things like, will I marry Ryan Scott?"

She turned the ball upside down and we all peered over her shoulder to look. A message floated up to the surface. "It is decidedly so," the message read.

"Yeeeeessss!" screeched Fliss.

If you didn't know, Ryan Scott is this boy in our class at school that Fliss gets a bit silly over. Yeee-awwwwwn!

"OK, OK, let me ask one," Frankie said. "Was it really an alien spaceship that we saw last week?"

Fliss tipped the ball over, and then back again. Up popped another message. "Yes," was all it said.

"Yo, Mystic Flisstic!" Frankie cheered happily. "I like what you're telling me!"

Me and Kenny exchanged looks, not quite so convinced about the magical powers of this plastic ball.

"OK, I've got one," Kenny said. "Is Fliss going to get eaten by an alien tonight?"

Fliss glared at her. "You can't ask things like that!" she said crossly.

"I just did," Kenny said. "Could the ball answer me, please?"

She winked at me and I grinned back. We were both REEEALLY hoping the ball would say yes again!

Fliss was looking dead miffed – she knew exactly what we were up to. But she tipped the ball upside down obediently.

I crossed my fingers as the answer floated up to the surface.

"Sorry, not today," was the answer.

"Ha ha!" Fliss said triumphantly. "See! The magic ball knows its stuff!"

"Not TODAY, it says," I pointed out. "So it still might happen tonight!"

Fliss shook her head, really chuffed that the so-called magic ball hadn't let her down this time. "I don't think so, girls," she said, smug as anything. "Anyone else got a *proper* question?"

We messed about with the ball for a bit longer, then had tea, then set up Frankie's bedroom for the night. No-one had mentioned wanting to sleep outside tonight – I wonder why?!

"We could even look through the telescope from up in your bedroom, Frankie," scaredy-cat Fliss suggested. "Just in case... in case we see anything scary. Then at least we'll be safe inside!"

"No chance!" Frankie said scornfully. "It'll be much more exciting out in the dark again!"

Fliss looked gloomy. "I knew you'd say that!" she said. "It was worth a try though!"

"Ooh, Mystic Flisstic predicts the future again!" teased Lyndz.

We got our sleeping bags and started laying them out in a line.

"Hey, you know what we haven't done for ages, don't you?" I said suddenly. "Squishy-poo fighting! Anyone fancy a quick game?"

"Top idea!" Kenny said, quickly stuffing her pyjamas and pillow into her sleeping bag to make a big floppy 'squishy-poo'. "Ready or not, here I come!"

Fliss screamed as Kenny whacked her round the head with the squishy-poo.

You've *got* to play this game! It's our very own invention where you stuff your sleeping bag with pillows, teddies, cushions, clothes, anything squashy – and then you go into battle with the others! The winner is the last one to fall over. It is AWESOME fun!

"Aaargh!"

"Help!"

"Gerroffff!"

Bish, bash, bosh! I managed to clobber Frankie from behind, then squishy-poo'd Lyndz right in the mush. Fliss made a surprise comeback and flattened Kenny with hers – so it was just me and Fliss left.

Biff! Pow! Wallop! I jumped on Frankie's bed to give me a better position – but then Fliss whacked my round the ankles and I lost my balance. Fliss, the squishy-poo champ – it was a miracle!

"I won! I won!" she yelped excitedly. "Eat my shorts, losers!"

After a few more rounds of that, and a slap-up pizza dinner from Frankie's dad, it was just starting to get dark. Yay! Even *I* was getting excited now.

We all raced out into the garden, and Frankie promptly grabbed the telescope to look through it first while Lyndz sat at the Mission Control desk, with a pen at the ready.

"What am I meant to be writing down?" she wailed. "Shall I put anything yet?"

"I haven't seen anything yet, dimbo!" Frankie said. "In fact, it's a bit cloudy tonight. Not very good for star-spotting."

It was ages and ages and *ages* before we saw anything. To be honest, it was actually getting a bit boring, looking through the telescope at Cuddington Hill just to see nothing, nothing and *still* nothing!

When it got to nine o'clock and we still hadn't seen anything or written anything down, it was my turn to peer through the telescope. "Maybe we should have another game," I said, putting my eye to the lens. "I mean, this isn't much fun, is it? And it's getting cold."

"Shall I write that down?" Lyndz asked eagerly.

"NO!!" everyone else said.

"Oh, let's look a little bit longer," Frankie begged. "We've got to give it a proper try! Otherwise we'll never know if we really did see something freaky last week!"

"Yeah, but…" I was about to argue, but then I stopped. "Hang on a minute," I muttered. "I think I've spotted something."

I moved the telescope slightly down. There it was again – small green lights in the sky. I blinked. It was definitely there – small green lights hovering in the sky, just around the place we'd seen the lights last week.

"OK, I see something," I said, trying to stay calm. "I'm definitely seeing something – green lights again."

The others all screamed in excitement. "Let me see!" Frankie said, trying to push me off. "Budge up, Rosie!"

"It's not very big," I said, my eye still glued to the lens. "In fact, it looks pretty small. I'm sure it's not half as big as whatever we saw last week. Here, see what you think."

Frankie practically pushed me over in her keenness to get to the telescope.

"Ooh, I see it, I see it!" she said excitedly. "It's moving – it's moving up and down. Now it's on the ground. Ooh – now it's up again. Well spotted, Rosie! Our aliens have returned!"

We all had a look. Fliss was practically hysterical. "I told you 'the plot thickens', didn't I?" she said. "That horoscopes book is AMAZING!!"

"Are we sure it's the same thing we saw last week?" I said doubtfully. "It looks much smaller – and the lights aren't half so bright this time."

"Well, maybe they're shape-changing aliens," Frankie said, waving her hand dismissively. "Maybe they've shrunk themselves so they can sneak around without getting spotted!"

"And maybe they've come back to get your coin – so they're going to sneak in to your house tonight!" Kenny said, eyes gleaming. "Which means only one thing..."

"RUN!!" squealed Lyndz. "Back in the house!"

So, just like last week, the five of us grabbed everything and dashed back into the house at the speed of light.

"Now do you believe it, Rosie?" Frankie asked, her eyes wild with excitement. "Now do you believe that we've seen something freaky?"

I just nodded, feeling dazed. "Yes," I said, with a gulp. "I think I do!"

CHAPTER SEVEN

Well, what can I say? To see flashing lights moving around on Cuddington Hill two weeks on the trot WAS pretty weird, and try as I might, I just couldn't think of a good explanation for it. GULP!!

If it had been difficult to get to sleep last Friday, this week it was a trillion times worse. I'd never seen the others so hysterical with excitement before.

"Why do the aliens keep coming back to Cuddington?" Frankie said eagerly. "Do you think they've been watching us?"

"Why US?" wailed Fliss. "I wish they'd leave us alone!"

"Maybe they've heard about five super-intelligent, gorgeous, funky beings in Cuddington and wanted a closer look," Kenny suggested. "That's us, by the way, in case anyone's wondering!"

"Maybe they want to borrow Fliss's horoscopes book," I said, nudging Kenny.

"Well, only if they're Virgos, I suppose..." Fliss said, taking me seriously as usual.

"I still think they might want their coin back," Lyndz said. "Maybe we should put it back on Cuddington Hill?"

"No way!" screeched Frankie. "That's part of our evidence, Lyndz!"

"I wonder if they're watching us right now?" Kenny said in a creepy voice. "They've probably got all this amazing equipment that lets them see through brick walls from miles away."

"They're probably checking out which of our brains looks the tastiest," I said, playing along. "Wondering which of us to chow down on first!"

Fliss screamed and dived into her sleeping bag head first!

"Oh, YOU don't need to worry!" Frankie said. "They're not interested in a load of fluff and hot air, Mystic!"

"Yeah, there's not enough there to keep even a baby alien alive!" Kenny said, prodding Fliss's sleeping bag with her foot.

Fliss's head shot out again. "I'll have you know that there's nothing wrong with my brain!" she snapped. "And what's more—"

"They're only teasing, Fliss," Lyndz said. "Hey, where's your mystic ball anyway? We can ask it what the aliens are up to!"

Fliss went a bit quiet while she thought. "I *think* I brought it in," she said doubtfully. "I was in such a panic to get inside, I..."

She looked wildly around the room, and then looked stricken. "Oh no, I think I must have left it in your garden, Frankie!"

All five of us looked at each other in silence for a moment. It was really dark outside now, and the thought of creeping around in Frankie's garden in our pyjamas looking for the mystic ball – which was black, anyway, so would be totally invisible out there – did not appeal to anyone.

"Does... er... does anyone fancy going to get it for me?" Fliss said hopefully.

I looked at Kenny. Kenny looked at Frankie. Frankie looked at Lyndz, and Lyndz looked at me.

"No WAY!" all four of us said at the same time.

"Not on your nelly," Frankie said, with a shudder. "I've gone off the idea of meeting an alien suddenly!"

"Oh, pleeeeeease!" Fliss begged. "What if it gets nicked?"

Kenny started to laugh. "Do you really think an alien who's managed to bring a spaceship here from outer space will want to nick a plastic so-called fortune-telling ball?!" she said.

"Well..." Fliss started, then shrugged.

She looked so sorry for herself, I gave her a cuddle. "Come on, then," I sighed. "Let's ALL go. We'll be all right together, won't we?"

"Will we?" Lyndz asked nervously.

"Rosie's right," Kenny said. "Come on! We'll be there and back in two minutes flat if we go now."

So – thanks to Fliss – that's how we all ended up creeping downstairs in our pyjamas and bare feet again.

Frankie grabbed a torch from the kitchen cupboard. "Ready?" she whispered, shining it under her chin, so her whole face went a ghostly yellow.

Fliss gulped, and nodded. "Sorry about this, everyone," she said in a loud whisper. "I didn't mean to—"

"Sssssssshhhhh! You'll wake Mum and Dad up!" Frankie said in a low voice.

"Not to mention letting the aliens know we're about to go outside," Kenny muttered.

Frankie fiddled with the key in the back door and eventually it swung open. Then, just at that moment...

ZAP!

The sky was flooded with light and we saw a huge dazzling flash of lightning right over Cuddington Hill. Just for a second, it was as bright as daylight. Then it went pitch black again, and there was a loud rumbling thunderclap which made us all jump out of our skins.

Frankie slammed the door shut again, and locked it, quick as quick. Her fingers were shaking as she did so.

"Er... I've changed my mind," she said. "Let's go back to my room – quick!"

We all charged back upstairs gratefully as the rain started pelting down outside.

"Wasn't that spooky?" Kenny said, once we were back in Frankie's bedroom. She ran over to the window and peered out. "Just look at it! There goes the lightning again!"

ZAP!

Fliss clapped her hands over her ears. She gets a bit nervous in thunderstorms. "Do you think the aliens have caused it?" she asked anxiously.

"Maybe," Frankie said, wrinkling her forehead as she thought. "Maybe there's lots of extra electricity whizzing round in the air from their spaceship – and it caused the lightning to strike in that very spot!"

"Oh, I bet you're right!" Fliss said, her eyes wide.

"I wonder if the aliens got blasted by it?" Lyndz said thoughtfully.

"We're gonna HAVE to go back up the hill," Kenny said. "This is all too freaky to be true."

I said nothing. I still wasn't sure the thunderstorm was connected to the lights we'd seen. But one thing was for sure – much as I hated to admit it, Fliss's horoscope book had been right again. The plot was *definitely* thickening now!

The next day, Fliss went charging out into the garden before she'd even had her breakfast. She was dead worried that her step-dad would be cross if she had lost her new present straight away – and more importantly, there were lots of questions she wanted to ask the mystic ball about last night!

When she came back inside, she was all smiles again. "It's quite dry!" she said happily. "It had rolled under a bush – look!"

"Now, if you were a real mystic, you'd have known that, of course," Kenny pointed out, but Fliss was just so relieved to have her ball back, she didn't care.

"Is Kenny going to get on my nerves all day?" she asked the ball, smiling sweetly across the table at Kenny. She tipped it over. "'No'. Oh, good, that'll make a nice change!" she said.

I caught Lyndz's eye and we both giggled. Kenny, for once, had no comeback. One-nil to Fliss!

We all ate our breakfasts mega-quickly so we could go exploring on the hill again. This time, Fliss went just as fast as the rest of us on our bikes as we pedalled furiously through Frankie's estate to get there. The night before all seemed too weird to be true, now it was daylight again. The flashing lights, and then that crashing thunderstorm that had come from out of nowhere... Freaky! I just couldn't work the whole thing out.

Once we got to the top, the five of us charged about like mad things. Lyndz was convinced that one area of grass was looking especially flat that day. "As if something really big had landed on it," she mused.

"Or the wind's been blowing it, maybe?" I said sarcastically, and she went a bit red.

"Mmm, maybe," she said, sounding disappointed.

We didn't find any more scorch marks, although we must have looked at almost every blade of grass up there. We didn't find any more strange green discs either. And there wasn't even a sighting of the M&Ms to give us a bit of a laugh. But we did find...

"Hey, look at this!"

It was eagle-eyed Kenny who spotted it. She was holding up something silver with a triumphant look on her face. "Come and look!" she yelled.

I felt my heart start pounding. What now?

But as soon as I'd had a closer look, I wasn't so excited.

"That's just a tag from someone's key-ring that's broken off," I said, handing it back to Kenny. "It's not anything alien – definitely not!"

The others were about to trudge off in disappointment, when Fliss grabbed it off Kenny.

"Hang on a minute, I recognise this," she said, staring at it intently. "I definitely recognise this. I've seen someone who has a key-ring just like this."

We all stared at it again. It was a silver oval

shape with a picture of a racing car on it.

"Loads of people must have one of those," I said dismissively. It was only an old broken bit of key-ring, after all!

"I know whose it is!" Lyndz said suddenly. "It's Dave's, isn't it? Caretaker Dave from school!"

"Yes!" squealed Fliss. "That's it. I KNEW I'd seen it somewhere before!"

"Yeah, he got it on holiday in Italy, didn't he?" Frankie said. "Turn it over, Kenz, what's on the other side?"

Kenny flipped the tag over. ITALIA, it said on the back.

We all stared at each other.

"It's definitely Dave's, then," I said, slowly. "Not many people in Cuddington have silver Italian key-rings, do they?"

"So what was Dave doing up here when he lost it?" Lyndz pondered.

Frankie's eyes went wide. "You don't think he... No," she said slowly. "He couldn't have been."

"WHAT?!" the rest of us yelled.

"You don't think he's been kidnapped by the

aliens, do you?" she asked, sounding horrified at the thought.

There was this terrible silence.

"Surely not," I said in the end, trying to sound confident. Inside my tummy, a hundred butterflies were going crazy. This was all getting far too creepy for my liking.

"But I really like Dave!" Fliss said, sounding on the verge of tears. "Why would they want to take Dave?"

"Yeah, why couldn't they take the M&Ms?" muttered Kenny. "The world would be a far better place without them!"

"Maybe his key-ring got broken when he put up a struggle," Lyndz said. "Oh no! I can't believe they've got him!"

"Hang on, hang on," I said, trying to sound calm, even though I was feeling as frightened as they were. "We don't know if he's been kidnapped for sure. Let's wait and see if he's at school when we go back on Monday. I mean, he could have just been walking his dog up here when his key-ring got broken and fell out of his pocket."

"Rosie's right," Fliss said in a wobbly voice.

"No point getting scared until Monday. And then we can all be terrified!"

"And if Dave HASN'T been kidnapped, maybe he knows something we don't," Frankie pointed out. "Maybe he saw the whole thing! Whatever, let's go straight round to that caretaker's shed on Monday morning to find out just what is going on!"

CHAPTER EIGHT

Normally I absolutely *hate* the first day back at school after the summer holidays. Is it the pits or WHAT? It's got to be one of the worst days of the year, if you ask me. But then, my mum thinks it's one of the BEST days of the year because she can chill out when we're back at school again. "Peace and quiet day" she calls it.

This year, going back to school felt a bit weird, though. Part of me was gutted about the thought of school work and tests and wearing school uniform, as usual. But part of me, for the first time ever, felt excited and a teeny bit scared. What if we went to assembly and Mrs Poole, our head teacher, told us that Dave wouldn't be our caretaker this year because he'd mysteriously disappeared at the weekend? Can you imagine?! I think Fliss would scream the school down in shock.

Anyway, SOMETHING was going on with Dave, we were convinced of it. He had to have some connection with the whole saga – and he was our best hope yet of finding out what was going on. I wanted to know all about it – we *all* did!

"You're in a funny mood today," Mum said as we had breakfast that morning.

I put down my spoon. "Am I?" I said innocently.

"Yes," she said, puffing hard on her cigarette. "You're very quiet. Anything I should know about?"

"No," I said, and started eating my cereal again.

"She's got a boyfriend," Adam said, kicking me under the table.

"No, I have not!" I said indignantly. Trust Darth Vader to stick his oar in!

"You have, I heard you talking to Frankie on

the phone about him." Adam was smirking his head off. He loves winding me up! "Dave, isn't it?"

"Ooh, dishy Dave, eh?" said Tiffany, putting on her make-up and earwigging as usual. She's the biggest gossip in Cuddington, after Fliss's mum. "When do we get to meet him, then?"

"Oh, shurrup, you two," I growled. You wouldn't think they're both older than me when they act like five-year-olds, would you?

Even Mum was getting interested now. "Is that true, Rosie? You are a dark horse! Have you really got a boyfriend?"

"No!" I practically yelled. "Dave is the school caretaker if you're that interested! And he is NOT my boyfriend!"

"Ooh, the older man! I see," Tiffany muttered, combing her hair in front of the mirror.

I glared at her but she was too interested in her own reflection to notice.

"So why did you keep going on about this Dave to Frankie, then?" Adam wanted to know.

"I..." I started – and then stopped again. If I said anything at all about aliens, I knew my whole family would fall about laughing. "Why do you have to be so nosey all the time?" I snapped at him.

"All right, that's enough bickering!" Mum said in a warning voice. "This is my peace and quiet day, remember? Now eat your cereal before it goes to mush!"

I gobbled down my breakfast, cleaned my teeth and ran off to school before I had to face any more embarrassing questions about Dave. It was bad enough them thinking that he was my BOYFRIEND, but if I so much as *mentioned* that we thought Dave had been kidnapped by aliens... well, I'd never have heard the end of it. I know I'm a cynic, but the rest of my family beat me hands down!

I met up with the others outside the school gates. Kenny was looking uncomfortable in her school uniform and kept tugging at the collar of her school blouse. "I'm sure this never used to be so itchy," she moaned. "Give me a pair of shorts and a T-shirt any day!"

"Do you know what? I asked the magic ball if this was going to be a good day today and it said 'No'," Fliss said anxiously. "I don't like the sound of that, do you? Mind you, last night I asked if the aliens were going to come and get me and it said yes to that – and I lay awake all night and they didn't!"

"Maybe the ball got a bit of water in it the other night at Frankie's," Lyndz suggested. "That might have made it go a bit funny."

"Or maybe it's just a cheap plastic toy with no magical powers at all?" Kenny said in a low voice. I think she was saying it to me rather than Fliss, but Fliss gave her the most horrible look so I think she heard every word.

"So it's Operation Dave this morning," Frankie announced as we walked up towards school. "Dave is the key to solving this mystery, so everyone keep their eyes peeled for sightings of our target. If we spot him – we confront him with the key-ring. And if we DON'T spot him, then..."

"Then what?" Lyndz prompted eagerly.

"Then... I don't know yet," Frankie confessed. "But remember, the Sleepover Club isn't afraid of anything!"

"Except aliens," Fliss said, looking a bit sick. "I'm very afraid of them!"

"And insects," I pointed out. "And ghost stories. And…"

"Thanks, Rosie," she said, glaring at me. "You're making me feel really brave, you know!"

Oops! At this rate, *everyone* was going to be in Fliss's bad books before school had even started!

When we got to the playground, all five of us were looking round eagerly, hoping to spot Dave. As time went on without a single sighting of him, Frankie started to get more and more excited.

"I knew it!" she was saying. "I knew it! He's gone! The moment I saw his key-ring up there, I knew something fishy was…"

Then Frankie's voice trailed away to nothing and we all turned to see what she was looking at.

"Oh," she said.

"It's Dave!" Fliss hissed, as we all spotted him at the same time. "So what now? Do we confront him?"

"Bagsy not me confronting him!" Lyndz said at once.

"Me neither!" said Fliss, looking horrified at the thought.

"There's something... different about him," Kenny said, screwing her eyes up as she stared at him. "He doesn't look the same somehow, does he?"

We all peered at Dave, who was emptying the litter bin in the playground.

"What do you mean, different?" I asked. He looked the same as ever to me. Tall, unbrushed hair, jeans, checked shirt... yep, that was Dave all right.

Frankie suddenly clutched my arm. "What if the aliens have taken over Dave's body?" she said dramatically. "He'd look a bit different then, wouldn't he?"

"Come on, he doesn't look THAT different!" I protested.

"Now you mention it, there *is* something funny about him," Lyndz said. "I think it's that expression on his face. He does look pretty weird, actually."

"So would you if you'd been taken over by an alien!" Fliss said, with a head-to-toe shudder.

Just then, Dave turned and caught sight of the five of us looking at him. He waved and smiled, and I suddenly felt sick with nerves. I was sure Frankie couldn't be right, but what if something HAD happened to Dave up on Cuddington Hill the other night?

"He's coming over!" squeaked Lyndz frantically. "What are we going to do? What are we going to SAY?"

"We're going to face the music," Frankie said firmly. "Try and act normal. Just try and act normal!"

Act normal? I was feeling terrified. And one look at the others told me they felt the same way!

We all held our breath as he walked across the playground towards us. For all Frankie's brave words, she was looking as sick as the rest of us.

"Hi, you lot!" Dave called. "Good holidays?"

I couldn't say a word. I just couldn't take my eyes off his face, wondering if that was really Dave the caretaker, or...

"Er... er... mmmm," stammered Frankie.

"Good result on Saturday for City, wasn't

it?" he said, turning to Kenny. His eyes seemed a really bright green in the sun.

Kenny gulped, blinked and then...

"Aaargh!" she screamed loudly, and charged off into the distance. And then, one by one, we all charged after her, leaving Dave standing there on his own.

"Did you see the way he looked at me?" Kenny gasped once we'd caught up with her. "His eyes looked all glassy – and I swear they've changed colour! They never used to be green, did they?"

My heart was thudding away inside me. I tried to be calm myself down – I mean, I *was* supposed to be the rational one, after all!

"Look, Dave is probably just the same nice Dave he's always been," I said. "Except now he must be thinking we've all completely lost the plot! Let's think about it for a minute. Just because we found his key-ring on Cuddington Hill doesn't mean ANYTHING, right? It doesn't prove there's any connection between him and those lights we saw, does it?"

There was a silence. No-one was looking at me.

"Right?!" I said, a bit louder this time.

"I know what I saw," Kenny said stubbornly. "Alien eyes, looking out from Dave's face. Bright green alien eyes. That's what I saw!"

"Remember ages ago when we were trying to matchmake Dave and Brown Owl, when we decided that Dave looks like Brad Pitt?" Frankie said suddenly.

We all nodded, remembering.

"Well, Brad Pitt has blue eyes, doesn't he?" Frankie said. She practically shouted it, she was so worked up. "And so did Dave – until today!"

With a sickening lurch, I had to admit she was right. "Which means that..." I began, not wanting it to be true.

"*He's an alien!*" Fliss and Lyndz both screamed at the same time, clutching each other in fright. "AAAAARGHHHH!"

CHAPTER NINE

I was starting to get *totally* freaked out by all of this. The green alien eyes were the last straw. People's eyes didn't just change overnight, did they? Not unless something really weird had happened to them!

As we walked into the classroom, I heard two familiar – and horrible – voices. The M&Ms! Ugh, just who I LEAST wanted to see right then! How sad that THEY hadn't been kidnapped by the aliens. Mind you, they were probably too disgusting, even by alien standards!

"Oh, look, if it isn't the lovely Pullover Club," said Emily yucky Berryman. "Or whatever it is they call themselves."

"Pushover Club, more like!" sniggered Emma Goblin-face Hughes. "Ha ha!"

"You'll be the Fall-Over Club if you don't watch it!" I said, sticking my tongue out at them.

"Yeah? Well we still haven't forgotten about your little waterworks display the other week," Emma said. "So I think it's you five that might just find yourself in a nasty little accident!"

"Or a nasty BIG accident!" sniggered Emily, giving us a mean look.

"Oh dear, how we've missed your dazzling wit," Kenny said sarcastically. "It's great to see you two again, though. Makes me feel *soooo* much better about myself!"

"Yes, I always feel particularly beautiful when I'm in the same room as the M&Ms!" Frankie added. "Not to mention particularly intelligent!"

The M&Ms looked cross at that. "Yeah, well..." Emily started – but that was all she managed to say.

"Settle down, everyone!" called Mrs Weaver,

our teacher. "Quiet, please! I hope you all had a nice summer holiday – I'd just like to remind you that this is actually a classroom and you're back at school now, where *I* do the talking!"

We all went quiet. Mrs Weaver is the sort of teacher you don't muck about with. Even Kenny gets a bit scared of her if she's in a bad temper!

"That's better," she smiled. "Welcome back. This morning we're going to start off with our new topic for the term, which is all about weather. I'm going to split you into groups and I want each group to find out more about a certain type of weather for a new display on the wall."

"Can we do thunderstorms?" Kenny said at once, her hand shooting up in the air.

Mrs Weaver smiled. "Nice to have such an enthusiastic group over there!" she said. "Yes, certainly. The other groups will be..."

Drone, drone, drone. I'd switched off my brain already. The other groups could have been finding out about fairies and Father Christmas for all I knew! I made the thumbs-up sign to Kenny and winked. Quick thinking from Mcklali, there!!

Lyndz rushed over and grabbed one of the encyclopaedias as soon as Mrs Weaver had sorted all the groups out. This was very handy! Using a school morning to find out more about that freaky thunderstorm!

"My granny used to say that thunderstorms were the noise of the gods playing marbles in the sky," Fliss said importantly.

Frankie gave her a withering look. "All grannies say things like that," she said. "Grannies live in a world of their own, half the time!"

"Thunderstorms happen when it's been really hot," I said. "I remember Tiffany doing a project about it at school. Something to do with lots of pressure in the air, or... Oh, I dunno! Anyway, what I'm trying to say is that it was dead hot and muggy on Friday, wasn't it? So it was probably that which caused the storm."

"Yeah, but it was so freaky, the way that lightning struck the very second we opened Frankie's back door," Lyndz argued. "Almost as if something knew we were there, and was trying to frighten us..."

"Maybe the aliens were trying to stop us getting my magic ball!" Fliss suggested, with a shiver. "Maybe..."

"Give us that, Lyndz," I said, grabbing the book off her. Anything to stop Fliss getting carried away! "OK, let's see what it says about lightning... Here we are. 'Lightning – A flash of light in the sky, during a thunderstorm'."

"We know *that*!" Kenny said impatiently.

"Give me a chance!" I said. "There's more. 'Caused by a burst of electricity, either between clouds or between a cloud and the Earth'."

"Or by the Earth and a spaceship, of course!" Frankie said solemnly.

The others nodded in agreement. "Just as we thought," said Kenny in a hushed voice. "We HAVE to tackle Dave about this. It all adds up!"

"I hope the aliens didn't get hurt by the lightning," Lyndz said anxiously. "It was a HUGE bolt, wasn't it?"

I burst out laughing. "Trust you, Lyndz!

Quick – someone tell Rolf Harris to take them to ALIEN Hospital!"

Fliss got out her horoscopes book. "Well, my stars for today say that I have to 'check the facts'," she said. "As usual, it's right! But how are we going to do that?"

"We can't just accuse Dave outright," Frankie said. "If the aliens know we've got wind of them, *we'll* be the next ones to get body-snatched!"

"We'll have to spy on him, follow him around," I said. "See if he's up to anything strange. Frankie's right – we don't want to accuse him. I'm sure he isn't, but if he really *is* an alien, then..."

"He could zap us on the spot," Kenny said cheerfully. "How was YOUR first day at school? Oh, you know, zapped by an alien, the usual..."

"Quiet, everyone!" called Mrs Weaver. "It's break time now. We'll carry on with this afterwards."

"Perfect timing," Frankie said. "Time for Sleepover Club to go undercover and 'check our facts'!"

* * *

It's got to be said – as a team, we're pretty good at finding things out. If you've heard about any of our other adventures, I'm sure you'll agree! Five brains are much better than one at solving mysteries – but even by our standards, this was proving a difficult nut to crack!

Lyndz suggested looking through the window of Dave's tool shed to see if we could spot anything strange. "WYou never know we might see another of those green discs, or see him communicating with the spaceship!" she said excitedly.

"What if everything's perfectly normal in there?" I said. "Should we go in and speak to him?"

"Oh, do we have to?" Fliss whimpered. "I don't want to get eaten alive!"

"Silly!" I said, nudging her. "We'll just ask him what he's been doing on Cuddington Hill, that's all. We can tell him we found his key-ring up there."

"Yeah, and if he's feeling guilty, I bet his face will be a picture!" Kenny said. "That'll totally give the game away!"

"Are we ready and steady?" Frankie asked. "Then let's go, gadgets, go!"

I felt a bit nervous as we approached Dave's tool shed. Nearly all of the weird things that had been happening could be explained away quite easily – but it still didn't make me feel any better. I just had this nagging feeling that something wasn't quite right.

Once we were near the shed, Kenny put her finger to her lips. The rest of us waited a couple of metres away while she crept up to the shed and peeped through the window. Then she turned back and beckoned us over, her eyes shining.

My heart started pounding. What had she seen?

Me, Fliss, Frankie and Lyndz crept up beside her and she pointed through the window with a shaking hand.

There sat Dave at a table, working on something... *something with a flashing green light on it*!

My jaw dropped. I just couldn't believe it. I stared at the others open-mouthed, not knowing what to say. Until now, I'd had an answer for everything – or almost everything. The lightning was just a storm, the key-ring hadn't proved anything, but now... now the evidence was staring us right in the face. Dave – or whoever he was – was mending part of the spaceship!

"Oh my goodness, I don't believe it!" Fliss said in a loud voice – so loud, that Dave turned round to see who was outside.

"Fliss, you idiot!" Frankie said. "Don't give the game away!"

"We've got to tell someone about this," Lyndz said urgently, her teeth chattering with fear. "Quick! Where's Mrs Weaver?"

Just then, the door of the shed opened. Dave!

"What are you lot up to, sneaking around here?" he said.

Seeing those bright green eyes again gave me goosepimples all over.

"N-n-n-nothing," I stammered. "Gotta go! Bye!"

"Look, there's Mrs Weaver!" shouted Kenny. "Quick, run!"

The five of us started to leg it towards her.
"What's going on?" shouted Dave after us.
"What the heck's going on?"

CHAPTER TEN

Thank goodness Mrs Weaver was on playground duty that day! The five of us pelted down towards her. I was feeling very frightened now. I'd never really believed in aliens before – but now I did, and I was very *very* scared of them!

"Girls! What on earth's the matter?" Mrs Weaver said as we charged towards her. "Is one of you hurt?"

"No, it's D-D-D-Dave!" Frankie said, stumbling over the word.

"What, Dave's hurt?" Mrs Weaver said. "Well, the speed he's running, he looks all right to me!"

"No, you don't understand," Kenny said urgently. "He's…"

"I'm what?" Dave said, as he caught up with us. "What is this all about? Why do you five keep screaming and running away every time you see me?"

"Must be those new contact lenses!" Mrs Weaver said to him teasingly. "Driving the girls wild, obviously!"

The five of us looked at each other. "Colour contact lenses, is that what he told you?" Frankie said disbelievingly. "Yeah, *right!*"

"What?!" Dave asked, sounding confused. "What do you mean?"

"We found this," Kenny said accusingly, holding the silver key tag out in front of him. "On Cuddington Hill." She raised her eyebrows meaningfully at him.

He took it from her. "Excellent! I wondered what had happened to that," he said, putting it in his pocket. "Thanks, girls – but you could have just given it to me in the first place, instead of this pantomime!"

"Is that it?" Mrs Weaver said. "Is that what all the fuss was about?"

"Not on your nelly!" Frankie said indignantly. "We haven't even got started yet!"

"He's an alien!" Fliss shouted, unable to hold back any more. "We saw him with Frankie's telescope – there were flashing lights up on Cuddington Hill, and then we found an alien coin, and..."

"And then there was this huge storm, caused by the spaceship!" Lyndz added. "And then we found Dave's key-ring!"

"*And* his eyes have turned green!" I said, pointing at them.

"AND we've just seen him mending the spaceship!" Kenny said, folding her arms across her chest. "Don't even *try* to deny it!"

I gulped as a strange expression came over Dave's face. What would he do, now the truth was out? Would he zap us? Turn us into aliens, too?

No – he started to laugh! A great big roaring laugh! He laughed so hard that he couldn't speak for a minute.

Mrs Weaver was looking totally baffled by it all. "Will someone please tell me what this is all about?" she asked. "Is it some sort of joke?"

Dave shook his head and managed to stop laughing. "That is the best yet!" he said. He practically had tears in his eyes from all the laughing. "What will you lot think of next?" he said.

I bit my lip. Uh-oh... Either Dave was doing a brilliant bluff, or the Sleepover Club might have made a bit of a boo-boo this time...

Kenny wasn't having any of it, though. "How do you explain that bit of the spaceship we saw you fixing in your shed, then?" she asked. "Let's hear it!"

"Certainly!" Dave said, grinning. "If you'd like to accompany me back to the shed, I'll show you exactly what I was fixing – and I'm sorry to say, it wasn't a spaceship!"

I was starting to feel a bit silly. Green eyes or not, it seemed that Dave wasn't really an alien, after all. We had just made ourselves look complete idiots – and to make it even worse, the M&Ms were listening in and they'd heard every word of it!

We traipsed back to the shed with Dave. Frankie, Kenny and Fliss still seemed convinced of the alien plot but one look at

Lyndz told me she was starting to have second thoughts too.

Then I heard a voice from behind. "Fancy still believing in aliens at their age!" it said. "What a bunch of babies!"

"Talk about stupid!" came another voice. The M&Ms of course. They were just loving this!

When we got to his shed, Dave pulled the door open. "There!" he said. "That's your spaceship! Not so scary now, is it?"

There on his desk sat an innocent-looking remote-controlled helicopter. And there on its top and tail were a couple of – you guessed it – green flashing lights.

"I don't believe it!" groaned Kenny. "That's our spaceship?"

"I reckon," Dave said. "Good, isn't she? I normally fly her in the day, but decided to fit a few lights on it so I could take her out for a night flight."

"Right," said Frankie wearily. "And we thought..."

There was a great cackle from the M&Ms who looked as if they were about to wet themselves, clutching at each other in fits of giggles.

"I had to pack up and go fairly early on Friday because of that awful storm," Dave continued. "Shame, 'cos I'd only just fitted the lights on and it seemed a pity to go home early on her first night flight and all. Still." He grinned at us. "Maybe next weekend, I'll be able to put on a longer show for you, eh?"

The M&Ms gave another scream of laughter, which was our cue to get out of there – as fast as we could!

"Sorry we thought you were an alien," Lyndz said, almost in a whisper.

"I'm glad you're not," Kenny said, adding as an afterthought, "I suppose."

"Well, I'm not glad," Frankie said, once Dave was out of earshot. "I'm totally gutted!"

"My horoscope DID say for us to check our facts," Fliss sighed. "That must have been what it meant. See? I told you my stars are never wrong!"

Kenny promptly tripped her up and she went flying on the grass.

"What did you do that for?" she shouted.

"Your stars didn't tell you THAT was going to happen, did they?" growled Kenny.

There was a bit of a bad feeling in the air. I think we were all really disappointed that the 'spaceship' had turned out to be a false alarm. And even worse, that the M&Ms had found out all about it, and knew what total idiots we'd been!

"We're never going to live this down!" I groaned, hearing them singing the theme from *Star Wars* behind us. "Oh, they're just loving this, listen to them!"

"Feel the force, Sleepover Club!" Emma shouted. "Feel the force – and feel the embarrassment!"

"Ignore them," Lyndz said through gritted teeth. "Pretend we can't hear them!"

But it was too late. Kenny had turned and started doing her 'Concorde' at them – where she put her arms out to the sides, screamed her loudest scream and ran at them, full pelt.

The M&Ms went from looking smug to terrified and immediately pegged it away from her. They know what Kenny's capable of when she's in a bad mood!

Two minutes later, Kenny was back, having seen them off. "That's got rid of those two morons!" she said, looking a bit happier.

Just then, Frankie stopped dead in her tracks. "Hang on a minute!" she said. "What was it Dave said? He took his helicopter out for the *first* time on Friday night, which means that..."

We all stared at her.

"Which means that it can't have been the helicopter we saw the week before," Kenny said slowly.

"Yes!" Frankie said excitedly. "So what did we see at first? Only the *second* lot of flashing green lights were Dave's helicopter."

"We did say it looked smaller on Friday, didn't we?" Lyndz said.

Fliss's mouth quivered. "Oh, no you don't!" she said. "We've just proved Dave isn't an alien, and it was just his helicopter we saw. Don't start making out we saw a spaceship again, *pleeeeease!*"

"Fliss is right," I said. "It was fun to think we'd seen a UFO for a while, but let's face it – it was probably just someone else's remote-controlled plane we saw the first time. Let's not go down that road again."

Kenny nodded. "Yeah, I agree," she said. "Sorry, Frank – maybe we've just been watching too many scary TV programmes lately."

Frankie shook her head stubbornly. "No way! I know there was something weird about it! The scorch marks on the grass, and that green disc..."

"Yeah, what happened to that, anyway?" Lyndz asked. "I'd forgotten all about it!"

"Safe and sound in my purse as always," Frankie said, digging it out of her pocket. "Here."

As she took it out, all five of us gasped at the exact same time. As she tilted it up to the light, there seemed to be a hologram of a creature on one side. And as she moved it back and forwards, I swear the creature started waving to us...

Well, your guess is as good as mine on that one. All I can tell you is that the disc definitely *didn't* have that hologram on it when we found it. No way! One of us would have seen it, without a doubt. So was it a trick of the light? No. The hologram was on the disc all day – and then the next day, it vanished again, just like that. Every now and then, when we're at Frankie's, one of us will get it out and fiddle with it, trying to see the waving creature again – but we've never seen it since.

Now that IS weird. Frankie, Kenny and Lyndz all swear it was a message from outer space. They're totally convinced all over again that we saw a spaceship that first time, although we've never seen anything except stars through the telescope since then. Fliss doesn't really want to know. It's scared her witless and she'd rather not think about it. Fair enough!

What was that? What do *I* think about it? Well, I really don't know. And maybe I'll never know! Do you have any ideas?

I'll tell you one thing, though. I've been reading up on space, and the sky is a big old place, you know. There are billions and zillions of galaxies and star systems all floating about out there. Surely our tiny little Earth isn't the only planet to have living creatures on it?

I'll leave you to chew over that one. It's keeping me awake at night, I can tell you. This is Rosie Maria Carromi Cartwright signing off. Sweet dreams!

33

Sleepover Club
Blitz

It's World War Two all over again for the gang when they get to experience a whole weekend in an authentic wartime house. No TV, no mod cons and no inside toilet – yikes! Not to mention scratchy knickers and heavy treacle pudding... And when an air-raid siren goes off in the middle of the night, there's creepy-crawlies in the air-raid shelter to worry about too!

The past's a blast with the Sleepover Club!

34

Sleepover Girls in the Ring

Roll up, roll up, the circus is in town! When Ailsa the circus girl comes to Cuddington Primary, the gang are up for some serious fun when they sort out circus lessons. But whose crazy idea was it to juggle jam doughnuts in Fliss's house? The Sleepover Club is in BIG trouble – and things just get worse when they discover that Kenny's monstrous sister Molly is going to have circus lessons too!

Stick on a red nose and cartwheel over!

35

Sari Sleepover

It's a Bonfire Night with a difference when feisty Asha arrives from India to stay with her aunt in Cuddington. Asha helps Frankie and her mates with their projects for Diwali, the Hindu festival of lights, and there's a crazy Indian sleepover and a whole lot of dressing-up fun thrown in. But trouble follows Asha wherever she goes – and when Asha's aunt loses a priceless necklace, the fireworks aren't the only things to go off with a bang!

Light the fuse
and run for cover!

36

Merry Christmas Sleepover Club!

Cinderella is the school panto this year! The question on everyone's lips is – who will get the lead role? Fliss is hopeful, but there's a dark horse in the race who might beat her to it. And surprises all round for Rosie when her mum finds her own Prince Charming! Will everyone live happily ever after, or will the curtain fall on disaster?

Ho! Ho! Ho!
for the Sleepover Club!

www.fireandwater.com
Visit the book lover's website

FREE GIFT ATTACHED!

Order Form

To order direct from the publishers, just make a list of the titles you want and fill in the form below:

Name ....

Address ....

....

....

Send to: Dept 6, HarperCollins Publishers Ltd, Westerhill Road, Bishopbriggs, Glasgow G64 2QT.

Please enclose a cheque or postal order to the value of the cover price, plus:

UK & BFPO: Add £1.00 for the first book, and 25p per copy for each additional book ordered.

Overseas and Eire: Add £2.95 service charge. Books will be sent by surface mail but quotes for airmail despatch will be given on request.

A 24-hour telephone ordering service is available to holders of Visa, MasterCard, Amex or Switch cards on 0141- 772 2281.

Collins
An *Imprint of* HarperCollins*Publishers*